Apple Countdown

Joan Holub   pictures by Jan Smith

Albert Whitman & Company
Chicago, Illinois

For Kristen Shaheen, a good apple—JH

To my dad, George Smith,
whom I couldn't manage without!—JS

Library of Congress Cataloging-in-Publication Data

Holub, Joan.
Apple countdown / by Joan Holub; illustrated by Jan Smith.
p. cm.
Summary: Rhyming text describes a school field trip to an apple orchard, where the students
count down all the things they see, from twenty name tags to one apple pie.
[1. Stories in rhyme. 2. School field trips—Fiction. 3. Orchards—Fiction. 4. Counting.] I. Smith, Jan, ill. II. Title.
PZ8.3.H74Ap 2009 [E]—dc22 2008031705

Printed in China
10 9 8 7 6 5 4 3 2 1 NP 22 21 20 19 18

Design by Morgan Beck

For more information about Albert Whitman & Company,
visit our website at www.albertwhitman.com.

"Field trip day! Hooray!" says José.

"Twenty apples with our names," says James.

"I see a tag for me," says Lee.

"Nineteen kids get on our bus," says Russ.

"I share with Mr. Yee," says Lee.

"Eighteen miles till we're there," says Claire.

"Eight miles, turn, then go ten," says Ben.

"Name seventeen things we might see," says Mr. Yee.

"An apple tree!" calls Lee.

"Sixteen steps to the gate," says Kate.

"Hi, Farmer Applebee," says Lee.

"Fifteen cars on a train," says Elaine.

"Five yellow. Five green. Five red," says Ted.

"Fourteen cows. Moo! Moo!" says Sue.
"That's twelve cows plus two."

"Thirteen ducks. Quack! Quack!" says Zack.

"Ten white ones and three black."

"Twelve rows of trees," says Louise.

"And eleven hives for bees."

"Yay! It's time to pick!" says Nick.

1. Hold an apple in your hand, pressing the stem against the apple with your index finger.

2. Twist upward.

3. Pull gently.

"Easy as one, two, three," says Lee.

"I picked small ones!
My sack will hold ten," says Ben.

"I picked bigger ones," says Caroline.
"My sack will hold nine."

"Mine are the biggest!" says Kate.
"My sack holds only eight!"

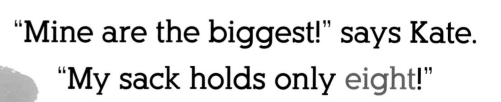

"My seven apples are green," says Christine.

"My six apples are red," says Ted.

"Want to trade with me?" asks Lee.

"An apple has five holes,
each with seeds inside,"
says Clyde.

4

"There are four seasons in a year," says Shakir.

"Winter branches are bare," says Claire.

"Spring flowers bloom, pink and white," says Dwight.

"In summer the apples grow," says Jo.

"Fall apples are ready to pick," says Nick.

"Three apple pies for us!" says Russ.

"How many slices are there?" asks Claire.

"Two times six, plus eight," says Kate.

"Two o'clock. Time to go," says Jo.

"Crunch crunch crunch crunch...

CRUNCH!"

"One lost tooth...for me!" shouts Lee.